W9-BLX-422

Dear Parents:

Congratulations! Your child is taking the first steps on an exciting journey. The destination? Independent reading!

STEP INTO READING® will help your child get there. The program offers five steps to reading success. Each step includes fun stories and colorful art or photographs. In addition to original fiction and books with favorite characters, there are Step into Reading Non-Fiction Readers, Phonics Readers and Boxed Sets, Sticker Readers, and Comic Readers—a complete literacy program with something to interest every child.

Learning to Read, Step by Step!

Ready to Read   Preschool–Kindergarten
• big type and easy words • rhyme and rhythm • picture clues
For children who know the alphabet and are eager to begin reading.

Reading with Help   Preschool–Grade 1
• basic vocabulary • short sentences • simple stories
For children who recognize familiar words and sound out new words with help.

Reading on Your Own   Grades 1–3
• engaging characters • easy-to-follow plots • popular topics
For children who are ready to read on their own.

Reading Paragraphs   Grades 2–3
• challenging vocabulary • short paragraphs • exciting stories
For newly independent readers who read simple sentences with confidence.

Ready for Chapters   Grades 2–4
• chapters • longer paragraphs • full-color art
For children who want to take the plunge into chapter books but still like colorful pictures.

STEP INTO READING® is designed to give every child a successful reading experience. The grade levels are only guides; children will progress through the steps at their own speed, developing confidence in their reading.

Remember, a lifetime love of reading starts with a single step!

BARBIE™ and associated trademarks and trade dress are owned by, and used under license from, Mattel. ©2023 Mattel.
www.barbie.com

Published in the United States by Random House Children's Books, a division of Penguin Random House LLC, 1745 Broadway, New York, NY 10019, and in Canada by Penguin Random House Canada Limited, Toronto.

Step into Reading, Random House, and the Random House colophon are registered trademarks of Penguin Random House LLC.

Visit us on the Web!
StepIntoReading.com
rhcbooks.com

Educators and librarians, for a variety of teaching tools, visit us at RHTeachersLibrarians.com

ISBN 978-0-593-57114-9 (trade) — ISBN 978-0-593-57115-6 (lib. bdg.)

Printed in the United States of America
10 9 8 7 6 5 4 3 2 1

Random House Children's Books supports the First Amendment and celebrates the right to read.

YOU CAN BE A PET VET

adapted by Elle Stephens
based on a story by Phil Williams
illustrated by Fernando Güell, Ferran
Rodriguez, David Güell, and Jiyoung An

Random House 🏠 New York

Brooklyn and Chelsea
play with the puppies.

Malibu sees Taffy.
She does not want
to play.

The girls are worried.
"Taffy looks hurt,"
says Malibu.

Malibu gives Taffy

a treat.

Taffy limps.

Her paw is hurt.

Malibu and Brooklyn
take Taffy to the vet.

There are lots
of animals.
"The vet is very busy!"
Brooklyn tells Malibu.

The vet is Dr. Clare.
Malibu tells her
what is wrong
with Taffy.

Dr. Clare checks
Taffy's paw.
There is a thorn in it.
It hurts Taffy.

Dr. Clare takes
out the thorn.
She cleans Taffy's paw.
Taffy feels better!

Dr. Clare asks Brooklyn
and Malibu to help.
They can learn
to be pet vets!

The next day,
the friends meet Nisha.
She works
with the vet.

The first patient
is a dog named Lobo.
"Hello, Lobo,"
Malibu says.

Lobo needs a checkup. Malibu helps Dr. Clare and Nisha.

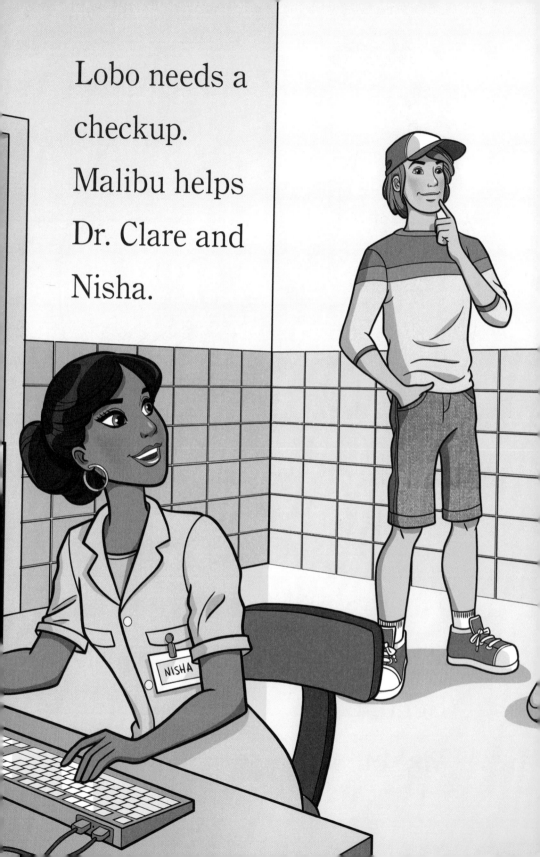

Dr. Clare weighs Lobo.
Malibu pets him
to keep him calm.

75.08 Lb

Lobo likes Malibu.
He lets her check
his teeth.
They look great!

Lobo is ready to go.

His owner thanks Malibu

for her help.

Some pets have to stay
at the vet overnight.
Dr. Clare shows Brooklyn
where they sleep.

A cat named Bertie
is there.
She is ready
to go home.

Brooklyn goes
to the waiting room.
She finds
Bertie's owner.

"Here is Bertie,"
Brooklyn says.
Bertie is so happy
to see her owner!

Next,
Brooklyn meets
a cute gray rabbit.
Her name is Fudge.

Fudge is at the vet
for a checkup.

Brooklyn gives Fudge
some grass.
"She is very healthy!"
Nisha tells Brooklyn.

Then Nisha trims
Fudge's nails.
Fudge is ready to go!

The next patient
is a dog.
She is wearing a cone
so she does not
lick a cut.

Dr. Clare says
the cut is healed.
Malibu takes off
the cone.
The dog is happy!

The last patient
is a snake!
Brooklyn and Malibu
learn all about snakes.

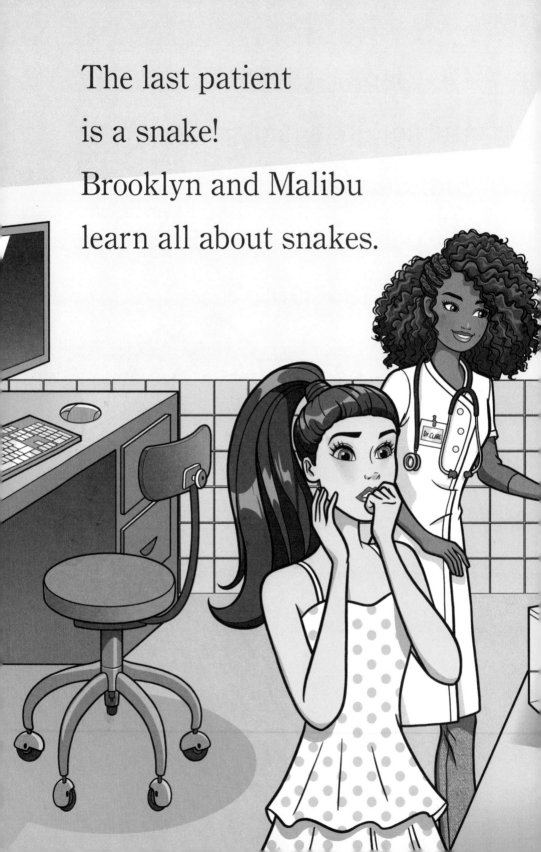

Nisha carefully
checks the snake.
She is healthy.

Dr. Clare thanks Malibu
and Brooklyn for their help.
"You can be a pet vet, too!"
she tells them.

Dear Parents:

Congratulations! Your child is taking the first steps on an exciting journey. The destination? Independent reading!

STEP INTO READING® will help your child get there. The program offers five steps to reading success. Each step includes fun stories and colorful art or photographs. In addition to original fiction and books with favorite characters, there are Step into Reading Non-Fiction Readers, Phonics Readers and Boxed Sets, Sticker Readers, and Comic Readers—a complete literacy program with something to interest every child.

Learning to Read, Step by Step!

Ready to Read   Preschool–Kindergarten
• big type and easy words • rhyme and rhythm • picture clues
For children who know the alphabet and are eager to begin reading.

Reading with Help   Preschool–Grade 1
• basic vocabulary • short sentences • simple stories
For children who recognize familiar words and sound out new words with help.

Reading on Your Own   Grades 1–3
• engaging characters • easy-to-follow plots • popular topics
For children who are ready to read on their own.

Reading Paragraphs   Grades 2–3
• challenging vocabulary • short paragraphs • exciting stories
For newly independent readers who read simple sentences with confidence.

Ready for Chapters   Grades 2–4
• chapters • longer paragraphs • full-color art
For children who want to take the plunge into chapter books but still like colorful pictures.

STEP INTO READING® is designed to give every child a successful reading experience. The grade levels are only guides; children will progress through the steps at their own speed, developing confidence in their reading.

Remember, a lifetime love of reading starts with a single step!

BARBIE™ and associated trademarks and trade dress are owned by, and used under license from, Mattel. ©2023 Mattel.
www.barbie.com

Published in the United States by Random House Children's Books, a division of Penguin Random House LLC, 1745 Broadway, New York, NY 10019, and in Canada by Penguin Random House Canada Limited, Toronto.

Step into Reading, Random House, and the Random House colophon are registered trademarks of Penguin Random House LLC.

Visit us on the Web!
StepIntoReading.com
rhcbooks.com

Educators and librarians, for a variety of teaching tools, visit us at RHTeachersLibrarians.com

ISBN 978-0-593-57114-9 (trade) — ISBN 978-0-593-57115-6 (lib. bdg.)

Printed in the United States of America
10 9 8 7 6 5 4 3 2 1

Random House Children's Books supports the First Amendment and celebrates the right to read.

YOU CAN BE A DOCTOR

adapted by Elle Stephens
based on a story by Lisa Rojany
illustrated by Mattel and Jiyoung An

Random House 🏠 New York

Malibu and Brooklyn
want to be doctors.
They visit a local
doctor's office.

They meet a nurse
named Mira.
Malibu and Brooklyn
are going to help.

A little girl
named Lily
is waiting with
her father.

Lily is nervous.

Her arm is in a cast.

Malibu and Brooklyn
tell her not to worry.

Lily smiles.

Nurse Mira comes
to get the girls.

8

"See you soon!"
they tell Lily.
The friends follow
Nurse Mira.
They are ready
to help!

Malibu and Brooklyn
wash their hands.
They put on
lab coats.

Malibu helps Nurse Mira
with an exam.
She says hello
to a boy named Oliver.

Nurse Mira checks
Oliver's weight.
Malibu writes it down
on his chart.

Then they check
Oliver's height.
"You are getting tall!"
says Nurse Mira.

Next, Nurse Mira
checks Oliver's
blood pressure.
She puts a cuff on
Oliver's arm.
She listens.

14

It is good.
Malibu writes it
on his chart.

Just then,

Dr. Vargas comes in.

She is ready

to see Oliver.

Dr. Vargas starts
Oliver's exam.
She uses a special tool
to check his ears.

Then the doctor
asks Oliver questions.
They talk about exercise
and eating healthy.

Malibu listens
with Oliver's mom.
She is learning
so much!

Brooklyn follows
Dr. Vargas
to another exam.

They check the chart
on the door.
Lily is the next patient!

Lily is ready
to get her cast off.

First, Dr. Vargas wants
to make sure Lily's
arm is healed.

Brooklyn takes Lily
to the X-ray room.
The X-ray will take
a picture of Lily's bone.
An X-ray tech
takes the X-rays.

"Great job!"

Brooklyn tells Lily.

Dr. Vargas looks
at the X-rays.
Lily's bone is
all better!

"Good news," says Brooklyn.
"We can take
your cast off!"

Dr. Vargas cuts the cast
with a special saw.
Then she uses a tool
to open it up.

Brooklyn helps take
off the cast.
Lily bends her arm
and wiggles her fingers.

Lily asks Brooklyn
and Malibu to sign her cast.

The friends help Lily
pick a special prize.
Lily chooses a
purple bouncy ball.

Malibu and Brooklyn love
helping Dr. Vargas.
"You can be a
doctor, too!"
says Dr. Vargas.